Fancy NANCY

and the Wedding of the Century

Written by
Jane O'Connor

Illustrated by
Robin Preiss Glasser

Cardiff Libraries
www.cardiff.gov.uk/libraries
Llyfrgelloedd Caerdydd
www.caerdydd.gov.uk/llyfrgelloedd
CARDIFF CAERDYDD

ACC. No: 03211815

For Cornelia and Rob G., who tied the knot on
September 21, 2013, and did indeed have the
wedding of the century. —J.O'C.

For Bob, for always
—R.P.G.

First published in hardback in the USA by HarperCollins Publishers in 2014
This edition first published in Great Britain by HarperCollins Children's Books in 2014

HarperCollins Children's Books is a division of HarperCollins Publishers Ltd.

13 5 7 9 10 8 6 4 2

ISBN: 978-0-00-756088-2

Text copyright © Jane O'Connor 2014
Illustrations copyright © Robin Preiss Glasser 2014

The author and illustrator assert the moral right to be identified as the author and illustrator of the work.
A CIP catalogue record for this title is available from the British Library. All rights reserved.
No part of this publication may be reproduced, stored in a retrieval system or transmitted in any form
or by any means, electronic, mechanical, photocopying, recording or otherwise, without the prior permission
of HarperCollins Publishers Ltd, 77-85 Fulham Palace Road, Hammersmith, London W6 8JB.

Typography by Jeanne L. Hogle

Visit our website at: www.harpercollins.co.uk

Printed in China

Weddings are always such glorious occasions.
(Occasion is a fancy word for special event.)
I have planned so many weddings and now finally...

...I am going to a real one!
"My uncle Cal called! He's getting married!"
Bree has been a flower girl twice. Right away
she asks lots of questions.

"Will the guests come in tuxedos and long gowns? Will it be at a fancy hotel?

And, most important, will you be the flower girl?"

I am almost 100 percent sure of that. But Uncle Cal wants everything to be a surprise.

"All we know is the bride's name. It's Dawn," I tell Bree. Dawn is a fancy way of saying sunrise. "With such a fancy name, the wedding is sure to be fancy, too."

The wedding is two weeks away. I dream about it day and night. I am packed long before we leave.

At last the big day arrives. Off we go!

I may shut my eyes for a moment or two to get a little beauty sleep.

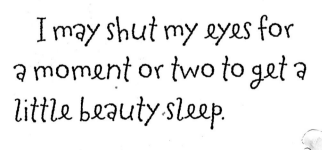

Ooh la la!
We arrive at the hotel. And I cannot believe my eyes.
It looks like a palace. A palace is even bigger than a castle.

There is a pool as large as a lake
and the world's longest waterslide.

I spend the afternoon at the beauty salon.

And *oui, oui, oui.* I am the flower girl.
(JoJo gets to hold my train.)

At the reception, which is fancy for party, there
is a band AND a DJ. We all dance the night
away. It is the wedding of the century!

All of a sudden I hear my mum calling, "Nancy, Nancy, we're here. Wake up."

Say what?

Was I dreaming the whole thing?

When I get out of the car I cannot believe my eyes.

We are in the wilderness! Suddenly
I have a terrible feeling that the wedding
will not be like the one in my dreams.

"I'm the flower girl, right?" I ask my mum.
"No, it's just the bride and groom," she says.

My mum explains that Uncle Cal and Dawn want
a wedding that is informal, non-traditional.
I realise right away those are fancy-sounding words
for P-L-A-I-N - plain.

"But I get to stay up until midnight at the reception?" I ask my dad.

"Actually, the wedding is in the morning, with breakfast after." My dad rubs his hands together and smacks his lips. "Mmm, pancakes!"

Breakfast? Breakfast is the least fancy meal of the day.

I try very hard to conceal my disappointment. That means I won't let anyone see how unhappy I am.

At least there is a waterslide.

JoJo and I meet Dawn. "I like collecting unusual pebbles," Dawn tells us. "Want to help me find some?"

"*Mais oui!* Of course we would," I say.

Ooh la la! Here is a big one in the shape of a heart. "It's translucent - that means you can see right through it," I explain to Dawn.

I give Dawn the heart pebble because she and Uncle Cal are in love.

"I will keep this forever," Dawn says. "Oh! The pebble can count as something new."

Dawn explains that brides like to have something old, something new, something borrowed, and something blue on their wedding day. "It's a tradition."

"But our mum said the wedding is non-traditional," I say.
"You're not doing the usual things."
Dawn smiles. "That's true, but I like this tradition.
And all I need is something borrowed."

"No problem!" I say.
"I can let you borrow something."

Dawn comes back with us to our cabin.
I find something absolutely perfect for her.

That night there is a party. I get to stay
up past midnight!

I never knew the wilderness was so noisy. An owl hoots.
Crickets chirp. At long last I fall asleep. It seems like only a
minute later I have to get up and get dressed for the wedding.

Of all the guests, I am the fanciest by far.

Here comes the bride. Dawn is beyond beautiful...
she is exquisite, breathtaking, ravishing.
Can you guess what she borrowed from me?

During the ceremony, we all weep a little because that is what you do at weddings. It's a tradition.

Uncle Cal and my new aunt Dawn kiss just as the sun is coming up.

I've changed my mind. There's nothing more glorious than a non-traditional wedding.

Last one in is a rotten egg!